THIS BOOK   BELONGS TO:

Other Kipper books

Kipper
Kipper's Toybox
Kipper's Birthday
Kipper's Snowy Day
Kipper's Christmas Eve
Where, Oh Where, is Kipper's Bear?
Kipper's A to Z
Kipper and Roly
Kipper's Book of Colours
Kipper's Book of Opposites
Kipper's Book of Counting
Kipper's Book of Weather
Kipper Story Collection
Little Kipper Collection

Thing!

Mick Inkpen

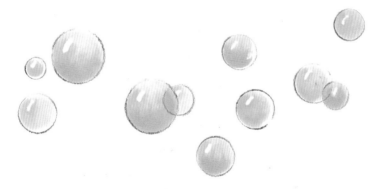

h
Hodder
Children's
Books

A division of Hodder Headline Limited

While Kipper was sorting out his box of toys he found a thing.

He could not remember what the thing was called, but he could remember what it did. It blew!

And when he found the special can that fixed onto the bottom, he remembered that it blew bubbles!

Just as the bubble mixture was beginning to run out, the doorbell rang.

'I bet that's Tiger!' said Kipper.

K ipper was right.
It was Tiger, with a
brand new sailing boat.
'How does it work?'
said Kipper.
'The wind blows it,
Silly!' said Tiger.
'Come on,
I'll show you.'

In the park, the breeze filled the sails of Tiger's little boat, and it sailed around the pond in a slow, graceful curve.

Then it got stuck.

They tried reaching it
with a stick, but the
stick wasn't long enough.

'Wait there!' said Kipper.
'I won't be long.'

A few minutes later, Kipper came back carrying the thing.

He tied it to the stick, wound the handle, and blew the little boat out of the lily pads.

'I'll run round and catch it!' said Tiger.

'Blow it a bit further,
Kipper! Just a bit
further!' called Tiger
across the pond.

Then he leaned out,
grabbed the boat, and fell
into the pond with a splash!

So they hurried home,
and Tiger sat in Kipper's
basket with a big, fluffy
towel wrapped around him,
while Kipper blew him dry
with the thing.

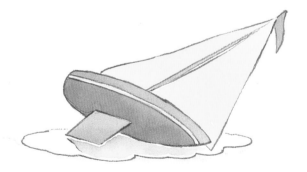

First published 2001
by Hodder Children's Books,
a division of Hodder Headline Limited,
338 Euston Road, London NW1 3BH

10 9 8 7 6 5 4 3 2 1

ISBN 0 340 78849 6

A catalogue record for this book
is available from the British Library.
The right of Mick Inkpen to be identitfied
as the author of this Work
has been asserted by him
in accordance with the Copyright,
Designs and Patents Act 1988.

Illustrated by Stuart Trotter

Printed in Hong Kong